D1491479

SPARROW'S PRAYER

BY *Roger Hutchison*

ILLUSTRATED BY *Ag Jatkowska*

South Dublin Libraries
www.southdublinlibraries.ie

LUCAN LIBRARY
01-6216422

beaming ✺ books
MINNEAPOLIS

Sparrow begins each morning by stretching his wings, whistling a morning tune, and thanking God for the new day.

But not today. Today Sparrow feels different. He feels restless. Anxious. Maybe it's the gray skies. Maybe he's hungry. Or maybe he didn't get enough sleep.

Sparrow tries to pray, but his words get tangled and knotted in his beak like old yarn and straw.

"Good morning, Sparrow," says Turtle, his mouth full of plump blackberries. "How are you this fine day?"

"Not great," says Sparrow. "I always begin my day with a prayer, but today I can't find my words. Can you help?"

"Hmmm. I don't pray with words. I pray by sharing. Have you ever seen so many blackberries?" Turtle says, turning toward the berry bush. "I want to bake a pie for Fox, but I can't reach the rest of the berries."

"I can reach the high ones," Sparrow says brightly.

"Wonderful!" says Turtle.

Together Turtle and Sparrow make the most fantastic blackberry pie and deliver it to Fox.

"Thank you for inviting me to help you, Turtle," says Sparrow.
"Fox's smile said it all!"

"Amen," says Turtle.

Sparrow notices his friend Mousie painting at the edge of the forest.

"Good morning, Mousie," says Sparrow. "Every morning I thank God for the new day, but today I can't find my words. Can you help me pray?"

"I don't pray with words," says Mousie. "My art is my prayer, but today I can't find the right color for the sky."

"Maybe I can help you," says Sparrow. "I know the sky well!"

Mousie mixes the paint and Sparrow flies the paintbrush into the sky until they find the perfect match.

"Thank you for your help, Sparrow," Mousie says.
"This is the perfect color!"

"There are so many beautiful colors in the world,"
says Sparrow.

"Amen!" says Mousie.

Sparrow sees his friend Buck spinning and hopping, twirling and stomping.

"Hello, Buck!" says Sparrow. "Is everything okay?"

"Is everything okay? Is everything OKAY?" Buck shouts. "Everything is magnificent! I am dancing! Join me!"

"Birds can't dance," says Sparrow. "And anyway, I don't feel like dancing today. I'm trying to figure out how to pray."

"Dancing is my way of praying!" says Buck. "Birds CAN dance. Come here, and I'll show you!"

Sparrow perches on one of Buck's antlers.

"Hold on!" Buck shouts as he kicks up his hooves and spins around.

Sparrow tries to hold on, but he is laughing so hard he lets go and starts swooping and gliding around Buck's head.

"That was fun!" Sparrow laughs. "Dancing with you brightens my day!"

"Amen!" Buck says.

As the sun goes down, Sparrow thinks about his day. He smiles, remembering baking a pie with Turtle and giving it to Fox. Helping Mousie find the perfect color for her sky made Sparrow feel closer to God, and he will never forget dancing for joy with Buck.

A beautiful rose glows in the light of the setting sun. Her peach-colored petals are open wide, reaching for the light with the last bit of summer energy stored in her dark green leaves.

Sparrow flaps his wings with excitement. "That's it!" he says.

"Turtle invited me to help make a special gift for Fox. Mousie invited me to help her with her painting. Buck taught me that anyone can dance, even a sparrow! And this beautiful rose . . . she, too, is praying!"

Fireflies sparkle and dance against the inky blue of the night sky. Each creature does what God created them to do. Each life is a prayer of thanksgiving, with or without words!

Sparrow's heart is full.

He spreads his wings and whispers "Amen."

Sparrow drifts off to sleep with a happy, thankful heart.

"O Lord, you have searched me and known me.
You know when I sit down and when I rise up;
you discern my thoughts from far away.
You search out my path and my lying down,
and are acquainted with all my ways.
Even before a word is on my tongue,
O Lord, you know it completely."

Psalm 139:1–4
NRSV

AUTHOR'S NOTE

Kneeling by my bed. Holding hands around a dinner table. Bowing my head in church. These are my earliest memories of prayer. It was formal, scheduled, and spoken.

When I grew up and started serving in a church, I learned a lot more about prayer.

I discovered that play was an act of prayer. Creating artwork became prayer. Focusing on my breath was a prayer—a prayer of gratitude for the One who gives us breath. Breathing as healing prayer.

We are created exactly as God intended, and we each have different ways of learning, communicating, moving about, and experiencing the world around us.

Spreading the colors across the canvas while I fingerpaint is a prayer of color and touch. I am talking with God, and I am not using words.

What senses might you use to pray?

• How could you pray with touch?

• How could you pray with taste?

• How could you pray with your ears?

• How could you pray with your eyes?

• How could you pray with your sense of smell?

You can also give prayers of thankfulness and gratitude by moving your body through dance, exercise, or other types of movement you enjoy.

Of course, I love all the characters in *Sparrow's Prayer*, but I especially love Buck and his joyful dancing. Do you have a favorite character? What did this character teach you about prayer?

Psalm 139 says it best: "Even before a word is on my tongue, O Lord, you know it completely."

Amen. Amen.

For Mousie, my childhood stuffed animal and
patient recipient of countless prayers and secrets.
—RH

Text copyright © 2023 Roger Hutchison
Illustrations by Ag Jatkowska, copyright © 2023 Beaming Books

Published in 2023 by Beaming Books, an imprint of 1517 Media. All rights reserved. No part of this book may be reproduced
without the written permission of the publisher. Email copyright@1517.media. Printed in the United States of America.

28 27 26 25 24 23 22   1 2 3 4 5 6 7 8

Hardcover ISBN: 978-1-5064-8159-3
eBook ISBN: 978-1-5064-8927-8

Library of Congress Cataloging-in-Publication Data

Names: Hutchison, Roger, author. | Jatkowska, Ag, illustrator.
Title: Sparrow's prayer / by Roger Hutchison ; illustrated by Ag Jatkowska.
Description: Minneapolis, MN : Beaming Books, [2023] | Audience: Ages 3-8.
  | Summary: When Sparrow cannot find the words to pray, he discovers new
  ways to connect with God without words.
Identifiers: LCCN 2022013614 (print) | LCCN 2022013615 (ebook) | ISBN
  9781506481593 (hardcover) | ISBN 9781506489278 (ebook)
Subjects: CYAC: Sparrows--Fiction. | Animals--Fiction. | Prayer--Fiction. |
  Conduct of life--Fiction. | LCGFT: Animal fiction. | Picture books.
Classification: LCC PZ7.1.H894 Sp 2023 (print) | LCC PZ7.1.H894 (ebook) |
  DDC [E]--dc23
LC record available at https://lccn.loc.gov/2022013614
LC ebook record available at https://lccn.loc.gov/2022013615

VN0004589; 9781506481593; DEC2022

Beaming Books
PO Box 1209
Minneapolis, MN 55440-1209
Beamingbooks.com

ROGER HUTCHISON is an author, illustrator, educator, and director of Christian Formation and Parish Life at Palmer Memorial Episcopal Church in Houston, Texas. In addition to *Sparrow's Prayer*, Roger is the author of seven books, including *My Favorite Color Is Blue*; *Sometimes: A Journey through Loss with Art and Color*; and *The Very Best Day: The Way of Love for Children*. Roger's ambition is to use art, color, and poetic language to communicate love and promote healing and hope in today's hurting world.

AG JATKOWSKA is an illustrator who lives and works in the United Kingdom. With a passion for creating whimsical scenes full of cute animals, soft colors, and various textures, Ag has illustrated dozens of children's books for publishers all over the world. In her spare time, she loves to discover new places and take long walks with her family. She is fascinated by different cultures, and loves film, theatre, and chocolate.

LUCAN LIBRARY

 01-6216422